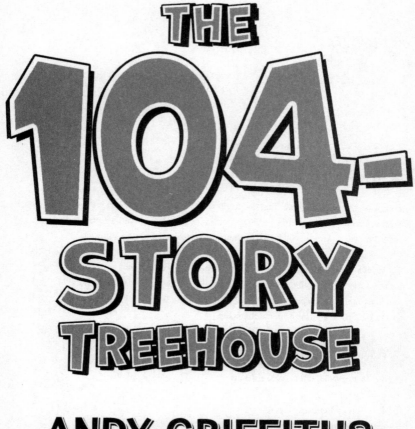

# THE 104-STORY TREEHOUSE

## ANDY GRIFFITHS

illustrated by Terry Denton

Feiwel and Friends • New York

A FEIWEL AND FRIENDS BOOK
An imprint of Macmillan Publishing Group, LLC
175 Fifth Avenue, New York, NY 10010

Our books may be purchased in bulk for promotional, educational, or
business use. Please contact your local bookseller or the Macmillan Corporate
and Premium Sales Department at (800) 221-7945 ext. 5442 or by e-mail at
MacmillanSpecialMarkets@macmillan.com.

Library of Congress Cataloging-in-Publication Data is available.
ISBN 978-1-250-30149-9 (hardcover) / ISBN 978-1-250-30150-5 (ebook) /
ISBN 978-1-250-23308-0 (B&N edition)

Book design by Rebecca Syracuse
Feiwel and Friends logo designed by Filomena Tuosto
Originally published as *The 104-Storey Treehouse* in Australia by Pan Macmillan
Australia Pty Ltd.
First published in the United States by Feiwel and Friends, an imprint of
Macmillan Publishing Group, LLC.

First U.S. edition, 2019

10 9 8 7 6 5 4 3 2 1

# CONTENTS

# CHAPTER 1

# THE 104-STORY TREEHOUSE

Hi, my name is Andy (*moan*).

A  Andy. (I just told you that!)

This is my friend Terry (*groan*).

LADYBUG LEVEL

stick insect

Are you okay?

stick ↑

Q What did the rock say when it rolled into the tree?

We live in a tree (*moan, groan*).

Well, when I say "tree," I mean treehouse. And when I say "treehouse," I don't just mean any old treehouse—I mean a 104-*story* treehouse! (It used to be a 91-story treehouse, but we've added another 13 stories.)

Q Which side of a tree has the most leaves?

So what are you waiting for?
Come on up!

Q How did the idiot get hurt raking leaves?

It's got a stupid-hat level,

Q Where does Dracula keep his money?

a money-making machine (that also makes honey),

a never-ending staircase,

Q How do shells get around in the ocean?

a Two-Dollar Shop (there's nothing *over* two dollars),

A  Taxi-crabs.

a Two-Million-Dollar Shop (there's nothing *under* two million dollars),

Why did the boy fall off his bike?

a refrigerator-throwing range (with a refrigerator-vending machine so we never run out of refrigerators),

a bunfighting level (with a bun-vending machine
so we never run out of buns),

Q  How can you say "rabbit" without using the letter R?

Mount Everest,

Q  What was the tallest mountain in the world before Mount Everest was discovered?

a burp bank,

a tangled-up level (where everything is really, REALLY tangled up),

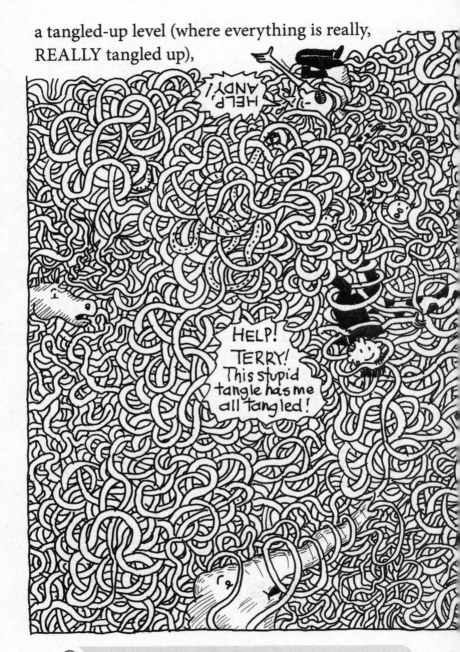

Q   What do snakes do after a fight?

A  They hiss and make up.

# a deep-thoughts thinking room,

Q   What is pink and can think?

a mighty fortress reinforced with extra-strong fortress reinforcer,

A    A brain.

and a beautiful sunny meadow full of buttercups, butterflies, and bluebirds.

Blue

Q  Where do butterflies sleep?

As well as being our home (*moan*), the treehouse is also where we make books together. I write the words, and Terry draws the pictures.

As you can see (*groan*), we've been doing this for quite a while now.

There are, of course, a lot of distractions in a
104-story treehouse (*moan*) . . .

Q    What's gray?

but somehow we always get our book written in the end (*groan*).

Q Why did the boy throw his clock out the window?

# ANDY'S ACHING TOOTHACHE

If you're like most of our readers (*moan*), you're probably wondering (*groan*) why I'm moaning and groaning so much. Well, the reason is I've got a really bad toothache.

A  Because he wanted to see time fly.

"Hi, Andy," says Terry, prancing toward me with a couple of lambs by his side. "What a lovely day it is in our beautiful sunny meadow full of buttercups, butterflies, and bluebirds!"

"No, it's not," I say. "It's a terrible day! I've got the most aching toothache in the world!"

What time do you go to the dentist?

"Hey, that reminds me of a joke," says Terry. "What time did the boy go to the dentist?"

"I don't know and I don't care!" I say. "My tooth is hurting!"

"That's right," he says, laughing. "Two thirty. Get it? Tooth hurty. Just like you!"

**A** Two thirty.

"Yes, I get it," I say.

"Then why aren't you laughing?"

"Because my tooth is hurting too much! It's hard to laugh when I'm in so much pain."

"That's too bad," says Terry, "because I love jokes! I reckon we should write a whole book of them."

"I'd love to," I say, "but with this toothache I just don't feel funny enough to write jokes. In fact, I'm not sure I even feel funny enough to write *this* book."

Q If life gets tough, what do you have that you can always count on?

"But we *have* to write this book," says Terry. "Otherwise, Mr. Big Nose will get mad!"

"I *know*," I say. "I just don't know how we're going to do it. This toothache is killing me."

"Hey, look up there in the sky!" says Terry. "It's a bird!"

I look up to where Terry's pointing. "I don't think it's a bird," I say. "That's Superfinger."

"No, it's not a bird *or* Superfinger," says Terry. "It's a *biplane*! And it's got a sign!"

Q Why did the plane crash?

TODAY!

FUNNY EVEN WHEN YOU DON'T!

NECDOTES, RIDDLES, RHYMES, ETC.

"A joke-writing pencil, Andy!" says Terry. "That's exactly what *we* need! It could help us write jokes, and it might even help us write our book even though you have a toothache. We should get one. Today!"

"But where from?" I say, just as a second biplane flies overhead.

"From a Two-Dollar Shop, that's where!" says Terry. "And we've got a Two-Dollar Shop right here in our treehouse!"

"You're right," I say (*moan*). "But I've only got one dollar."

Q Is an old 100-dollar bill worth more than a new one?

"Darn, I've only got one dollar as well," says Terry.
"Hmmm . . ." I say.

"Hmmm..."

 "Hmmm..."

"Hmmm..."

 "Hmmm..."

Q   What did one math book say to the other math book?

"I've got an idea!"
says Terry. "Why
don't we put our
two one-dollar
coins together and
then we'll have
two dollars?!"

"Would that even
work?" I say. "Is it
even possible? Do the
laws of mathematics
even allow such
a thing?"

"I think they do,"
says Terry. "But
there's only one way
to find out for sure.
Let's go to the
Two-Dollar Shop
and see if Pinchy
McPhee will let us
buy a two-dollar Joke
Writer 2000™ with our
two one-dollar coins!"

"I didn't know our sunny meadow had a videophone," says Terry.

"Of course it does," I say. "Most meadows do these days."

"I hope it's not Mr. Big Nose," says Terry.

"I'm afraid it might be," I say.

"I'm afraid, too," says Terry.

Q What demands an answer but asks no question?

I answer the phone. "Hello (*moan*), Mr. Big Nose,"
I groan.

"What's with all the moaning and groaning?!"
shouts Mr. Big Nose, scaring a flock of butterflies
fluttering close to the screen. "I don't have time to
listen to moaning and groaning! I'm a busy man,
you know!"

"I know," I say, "but my tooth—"

"I don't have time for explanations," interrupts
Mr. Big Nose. "And neither do you. Your book is
due today. It had better be on my desk by two thirty,
or else!"

"Well, we're running a bit behind," I say, "because of my toothache, but we've got a good idea to put lots of jokes in—"

Mr. Big Nose interrupts me again. "How about this for a joke?" he says. "What's big and red and gets bigger and redder the angrier it gets and then explodes if a certain writer and illustrator don't get their book to me by the deadline, which, just in case you've forgotten, is two-thirty p.m. today?"

Q  What's big and red and eats rocks?

"Um, beats me," says Terry.

"Me too," I say. "We give up."

"MY NOSE!" shouts Mr. Big Nose. "THAT'S WHAT! SO YOU'D BETTER GET IT DONE BY TWO THIRTY TODAY, OR ELSE!"

A  A big red rock-eater.

"Yes, Mr. Big Nose," I say, but he's already gone.

"I didn't think that was a very funny joke," says Terry.

"No, I think it was more of a *threat* than a joke," I say. "We'd better get to the Two-Dollar Shop and buy a Joke Writer 2000™ fast!"

Q   What's big and red and eats big red rock-eaters?

"Let's take our jet-propelled swivel chairs," says Terry. "It's quite a long way up."

Terry whistles and the chairs appear instantly.

We jump on.

"To the Two-Dollar Shop!" yells Terry as we take off at jet-propelled, supersonic swivel-chair speed.

Q   What rocks but does not roll?

# PENS, PENCILS, AND WRITING UTENSILS

We arrive at the Two-Dollar Shop. Pinchy McPhee is out front, waving his claws around and singing at the top of his voice.

A  A rocking chair.

Grand Sale! Grand Sale!
I'm having a great grand sale!
All items in my Two-Dollar Shop
Are priced at just TWO DOLLARS a pop!

Not one, not three
Not five: just TWO!
Just TWO dollars!
It's amazing—but true!

So—

"Excuse me, Pinchy," I say quickly (before he can start a third verse), "but isn't everything in the Two-Dollar Shop *always* only two dollars?"

"Of course," says Pinchy. "But today is a *grand sale*, so two dollars is an extra-special price!"

Q  What did the bird say at the sale?

Terry frowns. "But if everything is *normally* two dollars and your *sale* price is two dollars, how is today different from any other day?"

"Because any other day is *not* a grand sale and today *is*!" says Pinchy, getting slightly crabby and waving his claws dangerously close to us.

We nod and step into the shop before he can get any crabbier.

"Wow!" says Terry. "This shop has everything! Check it out!"

SMALL RIVER $2

Q What do you call a sheep without legs?

A A cloud.

"Hey, look at this electric banana," says Terry. "It's only *two* dollars!"

"And this giant glow-in-the-dark marshmallow is bigger than my *head*," he says. "And it's only two dollars, too!"

Q   What's yellow and smells like bananas?

"And check out this model of our treehouse!" says Terry. "We could buy it and have a treehouse in our treehouse!"

"And there's also a model of the model of the treehouse!" he says. "We could have a treehouse in our treehouse in our treehouse!"

A Monkey vomit.

"Oh, wow!" says Terry, picking up a golden toilet seat. "Here's that solid-gold toilet seat we've always wanted—and it's only two dollars as well! Can we get it, Andy? Please, please, please, please, please, please? A solid-gold toilet seat would solve *all* our problems!"

"No, it wouldn't," I say. "We came to buy a Joke Writer 2000™ and that's what we're going to do. *That* is going to solve all our problems."

Q  Why did Tigger go to the bathroom?

"Oh, yeah, I forgot," says Terry, turning to Pinchy. "Excuse me, Pinchy, do you sell pencils?"

"Of course I do," says Pinchy. He takes a deep breath and starts singing.

♫♫ I have pens and pencils and writing utensils
Of all sorts right here in my store:
I have dip pens and gel pens and ballpoints
And crayons and markers galore! ♫♫

A   He was looking for his friend, Pooh.

I have a pen you can use as a lipstick,
And a pen that can write underwater,
And a pen for writing excuses,
In case you haven't done something you oughta.

I have a pen that can write upside down
Like the astronauts took into space,
And a pen you can use to write notes on your hand.
Or—if you prefer—on your face.

Q  Where do astronauts park their spaceships?

And here is a pen,
My pen-loving friends,
That comes with a little night-light.
You can write in the night
For as long as you like
Because the little night-light is quite bright!

CONE OF DARKNESS

A   Parking meteors.

And here is a pen
With a fan on the end—
You can use it to write when it's hot.
And it also comes with a heater attached
So you can write whether it's hot or it's not.

Q  What did one pencil say to the other pencil?

I have a pen that writes with invisible ink,
That's particularly good for spies,
And a pen that always tells the truth
And one that will only write lies.

I have a pen that changes into a car,
And one that turns into a jet.
And a pen with fur and ears and a tail—
It's the next best thing to a pet!

A   "You're looking sharp!"

So, as you can see, I have all you could need,
And no pen is priced over two dollars.
I have bargains galore in my two-dollar store
For authors, illustrators, and scholars!

"So, what will it be?" says Pinchy. "What type of pen or pencil would you like?"

"A Joke Writer 2000™, please," I say.

Q  What did the pen say to the pencil?

"I'm afraid I'm clean out of them," says Pinchy.
"They've been very popular this morning, thanks to
my biplane advertising campaign. But not to worry,
I have lots of other wonderful pens and pencils."

He takes a deep breath.

"Uh-oh," whispers Terry. "I think he's going to
sing again."

"No, it's okay, Pinchy," I say quickly. "We really
just want a Joke Writer 2000™."

"I guess you could try Fancy Fish's Two-Million-Dollar Shop," says Pinchy. "He might have one."

"Thanks, Pinchy!" says Terry. "We'll go there right now."

We fly to the Two-Million-Dollar Shop as fast as we can without stopping.

Q What's a plumber's favorite song?

The Two-Million-Dollar Shop is much better than the Two-Dollar Shop, but, of course, all the stuff is a lot more expensive.

"Wow!" says Terry. "This shop has everything! Check it out!"

Q Why do birds fly south?

"Greetings, my good fellows," says Fancy Fish.
"Welcome to my two-million-dollar emporium.
How may I be of service?"

"We'd like to buy a Joke Writer 2000™, please,"
I say.

Q What's green, sticky, and smells like eucalyptus?

"An excellent choice, if I may say so, sir," says Fancy Fish. "The Joke Writer 2000™ is a wonderful pencil and very well-priced at only two million dollars. They have proved enormously popular—in fact, this is my last one." He places it on the counter in front of us.

Joke Writer 2000™

JOKE WRITER 2000™

$2,000,000

I wish I had one of those. I could write some really funny fly jokes.

Fly →

A  Koala vomit.

"We'll buy it!" says Terry.

"Hang on, not so fast," I say. I turn to Fancy Fish. "Will you excuse me for a moment while I consult with my colleague?"

"Of course," says Fancy Fish.

I draw Terry aside.

"What's the matter, Andy?" he says. "It's exactly what we need."

"Yes," I say, "but it costs two million dollars and we only have two one-dollar coins!"

Q   Where do fish go for their vacation?

"Oh, yeah," says Terry. "That's too bad . . . unless . . . unless . . ."

"Unless what?" I say.

"Unless we use our money-making machine to *make* one million, nine hundred and ninety-nine thousand, nine hundred and ninety-eight dollars? Then we can add our two one-dollar coins and we'll have two million dollars!"

"Brilliant!" I say. "Why didn't *I* think of that?"

"Because you've got a toothache, that's why."

"*Ouch!*" I say. "Thanks for reminding me."

I turn to Fancy Fish. "Hold that Joke Writer 2000™ —we'll be right back!"

"Well, I'll try," says Fancy Fish, "but I can't guarantee anything. At this price it won't last long."

CHAPTER 4

# THE 100-BEAR BUNFIGHT

We hurry to the money-making machine.

"How do you turn this thing on?" I say.

"Easy," says Terry. "You just flick the 'honey/money' switch to 'money' and then press the 'on' button—like this."

The machine whirs into action and money starts flying everywhere.

"Making money is fun!" says Terry as he jumps around excitedly, snatching money out of the air.

"Be careful," I say. "Don't bump the 'honey/money' switch."

Q   What is harder to catch the faster you run?

"Oops," says Terry as he slips backward and bumps into the HONEY/MONEY switch!

The machine makes a weird growling, gluggy sound as it switches from making money to making . . .

A Your breath.

Q What did the bee say to the flower?

A "Hello, honey!"

Before we know it, we're up to our knees in honey! It's pouring out of the machine in great sticky waves.

"Terry, you idiot!" I yell. "You bumped into the 'honey/money' switch."

"I'm sorry," says Terry. "But it's okay, I've turned the machine off now."

"Then why is it still making that weird growling sound?" I say.

"That's not the machine," says Terry. "That's *actual* growling—I think it's coming from all those bears!"

"Bears?" I say.

"Yes," says Terry. "Look!"

Q How do bears keep their caves cool?

A Bear-conditioning.

"Oh, no!" says Terry. "This is *bad*!"

"No," I say, "it's actually *good*—they're eating all the honey!"

"But what about when there's no more honey left?" says Terry. "Then the bears will eat *us*!"

"Not these ones," I say. "These are obviously *honey*-eating bears, not human-eating bears."

"I think they must be bun-eating bears as well," says Terry, pointing up at the bunfighting level. "Look!"

"Uh-oh!" I say. "They're not just *eating* the buns—they're throwing them as well . . . WATCH OUT!!!"

I take cover, but Terry is too slow. One of the buns hits him in the head and knocks him over.

Terry jumps back up. "Right!" he says. "This means war!"

"Yeah," I say. "If it's a bunfight they want, then it's a bunfight they'll get!"

Q   What do you call a bear with no teeth?

We scoop up the buns the bears have thrown at us and start hurling them back.

Q When are people like bears?

A When they're bearfoot.

Buns of all types are flying through the air in all directions. Hot cross buns, cold cross buns, Boston buns, cinnamon buns, cream buns, currant buns, out-of-date buns, hamburger buns, hot-dog buns, refrigerator buns . . . hang on, REFRIGERATOR BUNS?!

There's no such thing as *refrigerator buns*!
The bears are throwing *actual* refrigerators!

"Cut it out, you bears!" I say. "Fridge-throwing is totally against the rules of bunfighting! Look at the sign!"

Q What's black and white, black and white, black and white?

"Maybe bears can't read," says Terry.

"I think you're right," I say. "We'd better get to the fortress—and fast—before we get flattened by a flying fridge!"

"Or four flying fridges," says Terry, as four flying fridges fly toward us. "Flee!"

We make it just in time. Fridges smash into the wall of our fortress, but because it's reinforced with extra-strong fortress reinforcer, it has no trouble withstanding the ferocious fridge attack.

A A panda bear rolling down a hill.

"How long do you think they'll keep it up for?" says Terry.

"Who knows?" I say. "They could go on forever . . . or until the refrigerator-vending machine runs out of refrigerators—whichever comes first, I guess."

"If only Jill was here," says Terry. "She could talk to the bears and ask them to stop throwing fridges."

"Hey, I know," I say, "let's call Jill!"

"Good idea, Andy!" says Terry.

Q Why did the bear fall off his bike?

A Because his mother threw a fridge at him.

Within moments, Jill zooms down out of the sky and lands her flying-cat sleigh safely inside the walls of our fortress.

"I heard your call and came as fast as I could," she says. "What are all these bears doing in the treehouse—and why are they throwing refrigerators at you?"

Q  Why did the bear fail his math test?

"Well," I say, "we were using the money-making machine to make some money, but Terry knocked the switch to 'honey' and then the bears came to eat it all up. And then they started throwing buns."

"And fridges," says Terry. "Can you make them stop?"

"Well, I'll try," says Jill. "Bears can be very stubborn, but I'll have a word with them."

Q Why did the fridge fall off its bike?

The bears put the fridges down and look up at Jill.

"I'm very disappointed in you bears," she says. "This is no way to behave when you're a guest in somebody's treehouse."

One of the bears steps forward and growls quietly up at Jill.

"That must be their spokesbear," says Terry.

Jill turns to us. "The bears say they're very sorry," she says.

"That's okay," I say.

"Yeah," says Terry. "It's all right. The bunfight was actually a lot of fun. It was just the fridges we had a problem with."

"You know," Jill says to the bears, "it's almost winter, so you should be settling down to some serious hibernation. How about you all go home now and I'll come to your cave later, tuck you in, and read you a nice bear-time story, perhaps even *The 104-Story Treehouse*?"

The bears obviously like Jill's idea. They start jumping around excitedly, high-pawing one another.

Ｑ Why did the fridge fall out of the tree?

"Bears *love* their bear-time stories," explains Jill.

The spokesbear taps Jill on the shoulder and growls in her ear.

Jill turns to us and says, "He wants to know if there are any bears in your story?"

"Only about one hundred!" I say.

The bears all start growling excitedly, and Jill translates for us.

"They said would you please come, too, and read it with me?"

"Sure," says Terry. "We can do that."

"Yes," I say. "But we have to finish it first."

"Well, we'd better get going then," says Jill, "and let you get on with it."

She climbs into her flying-cat sleigh and calls to the bears. "Follow me! My cats and I will show you the quickest way home."

"See you all later!" shouts Terry. "And thanks for eating all the honey—it would have taken us ages!"

Q  What sort of stories do bears like best?

# CHAPTER 5

# IF ONLY . . .

"Well, if we're going to have this book ready to read to the bears, we'd better get started," says Terry.

"I know!" I say (*moan*). "But my tooth is still killing me. I hope the money-making machine made enough money for us to buy the Joke Writer 2000™."

A   Furry tales.

I pick up a handful of sticky money and start counting.

"One . . . five . . . two . . . (*groan*) . . ."

"Andy?" says Terry.

"Shush," I say, "I'm trying to concentrate. Seven . . . five . . . nine . . . (*moan*) . . ."

Why didn't the cannibals eat the clown?

"Um, Andy?"

"Not now, Terry. Ten . . . eleventeen—"

"ANDY!!!" shouts Terry.

"Stop interrupting me!" I say. "You've made me lose my place! I'm going to have to start all over again!"

"Sorry," says Terry. "But that's what I wanted to talk to you about. The readers and I were wondering if you could count a bit faster . . . and in the right order."

"I'm counting as fast—and as well—as I can!" I say.

"But it's taking *forever*," says Terry. "I think you might need a little help. I'm going to the stupid-hat level—I'll be right back."

Q  What do penguins wear on their heads?

A few minutes later Terry returns with a stupid-looking hat, which he puts on my head.

"I don't want to wear this stupid hat," I say.

"I know it looks stupid," says Terry, "but it will make you smart: it's a stupid-looking, superfast counting hat."

"Well, in that case," I say, "let the superfast counting begin!"

THE DAY I PUT ON THE STUPID-LOOKING, SUPERFAST COUNTING HAT AND COUNTED FASTER THAN ANY PERSON HAS EVER COUNTED IN THE ENTIRE HISTORY OF COUNTING...EVER!

1. 2. ...3...4...5...
15...16...17..18

33...

520

...8...9...10...11...12...13...14...

...20...21...22...23...24...

41...65...130...260...

1,040...3,072½...

2,20,604...

506,321...

999,996...

Pretty soon I've counted every last bit of money. "We have one million, nine hundred and ninety-nine thousand, nine hundred and ninety-six dollars," I say.

"Darn!" says Terry. "We're four dollars short."

When I point up it's bright, but when I point down it's dark. What am I?

"Only *two* dollars short, actually," I say. "Remember, we've also got *my* one-dollar coin and *your* one-dollar coin."

"In that case," says Terry, "all we have to do is use the money-making machine to make two more dollars."

"We can't!" I say. "The 'honey/money' switch is all glugged up with honey and won't flick back to 'money.'"

"Oh, no!" says Terry. "How are we going to pay for the Joke Writer 2000™ now?"

"I don't know," I say. "I can't think of anything. My tooth hurts too much."

"What about the burp bank?" says Terry. "We must have at least *twenty* spare burps in there. We could use them!"

"We can't pay in burps," I say.

"Why not?" says Terry.

"Because then everybody would be doing it," I say. "And it would be disgusting."

"That's too bad," says Terry. "I think paying for things with burps would be cool."

"Maybe we should try the deep-thoughts thinking room," says Terry. "That might help. Remember how last time we were there I had the thought that it might be nice to have ice cream with sausages for breakfast and then we did and I was right?"

"Yeah," I say, "that was a good deep thought. Let's try it."

Two sausages are on a grill. One says, "Wow, is it hot in here or is it just me?" What does the other one say?

We fly to the deep-thoughts thinking room and settle into our deep-thoughts thinking positions.

"Hmmm (*moan*) . . ."

"Got anything yet, Andy?"

"Nope. You?"

"Not yet . . ."

What happened to Einstein when he took a shower?

"Hang on (*groan*), I
think I'm having a deep
thought!"

"Hey, me too!
What's yours?"

"It's about how much
my tooth is aching . . ."

"Mine's about sausages . . ."

A   He was brainwashed.

Q  What does a shark eat with peanut butter?

"I've got it!" says Terry. "Sausages and sausages *and* sausages! What did you come up with?"

"Nothing," I say. "All I can think about is how much my tooth aches (*moan*). And how it's all your fault! If only you'd listened to me when I said don't bump the 'honey/money' switch on the money-making machine. But you went and bumped it anyway, and now we don't have enough money to buy a Joke Writer 2000™!"

"Look on the bright side," says Terry. "We got lots of honey."

Q  What has teeth but no mouth?

"But we didn't *need* honey," I say. "We need a Joke Writer 2000™! And the only reason we need that is because I have a toothache, and my toothache is *your* fault, too!"

"How is *your* toothache *my* fault?" says Terry.

"Remember that marshmallow-flavored toothpaste you invented for people who hate peppermint-flavored toothpaste?"

"Yes," says Terry. "What about it?"

I think you'll be needing this.

"Well, it didn't prevent tooth decay," I say. "It *caused* it!"

"That's not my fault," says Terry. "I put a warning on the tube. Look—it's right here!"

How do you clean a dirty tuba?

JERRY'S MARSHMALLOW-FLAVORED TOOTHPASTE

FOR PEOPLE WHO HATE PEPPERMINT-FLAVORED TOOTHPASTE

INGREDIENTS: POLLY-WOLLY-DOODAH-HYDROXY-FOXY-ETHYL-METHYL-KETONE-DICHLORO-BERYLLIUM-BORON-MORON-LYTHIATE(1%) MARSHMALLOWS (99%)

WARNING: MAY NOT ACTUALLY CLEAN TEETH. MAY NOT BE SUITABLE FOR HUMANS. MAY NOT ESPECIALLY BE SUITABLE FOR ANYONE CALLED ANDY.

"But why would you invent such a dumb toothpaste in the first place?" I say. "If only you'd listened to me when I said NOT to invent a really dumb toothpaste! In fact, pretty much *all* of our problems could be avoided IF ONLY YOU WOULD LISTEN TO WHAT I SAY!!!"

"Hey, that gives me an idea for a song," says Terry.

If only I'd listened to Andy,
I would never have done anything wrong.
If only I'd listened to Andy,
I wouldn't be singing this song.

But I didn't listen to Andy
And now he is groaning in pain.
Oh, why am I always so stupid?
Again and again and again?!

A   Pop music.

Like the time I married a mermaid,
Who was actually a monster from the sea,
And she practically ended up eating
Both my good friend Andy and me!

Which part of a mermaid weighs the most?

And the time **I** used the sharks in the
    shark tank
**To** wash my underpants.
And the time **I** left open the ant-farm gate
And let out all of the ants.

**A**  Her scales.

If only I'd listened to Andy,
I wouldn't have invented a machine
To write and draw our books for us
That turned out to be really mean.

How do snails get their shells so shiny?

And if only I hadn't trained Ninja Snails—
Oh, hang on, they worked out okay!
Even though it took them 100 years,
They ended up saving the day.

A   They use snail polish.

But I didn't listen to Andy
When he warned me about spying cows!
And then their stupid, dumb mooo-vie
Was much more successful than ours.

Q What do you call a cow's bedtime stories?

♪♪
If only I'd listened to Andy
When we were using our machine
    to make money,
I wouldn't have bumped the switch   ♪♪
And flooded the treehouse with honey.

And **I** would NEVER have invented
   a toothpaste
That was 99 percent candy.
**I'm** so sorry for all the dumb things
   **I** have done.
Oh, **I** feel so bad for poor Andy.

Q   How do you spell candy in two letters?

If only I could think of a way
To get that tooth out of his head,
Why, I'd pull it right out in an instant
And he could leave it at night by his bed.

The tooth fairy could come and collect it
And leave a gold coin in its place
And Andy would feel so much better—
It would put a huge smile on his face!

Q  Why are tooth fairies so smart?

He'd say, "Terry, you're not such a dum-dum!
You've done something right for a change!
We can take all this money back to the shop
And get the pencil we need in exchange!"

"THAT'S IT! HEY, ANDY! I'VE GOT A WAY TO SOLVE ALL OUR PROBLEMS AND MAKE EVERYTHING RIGHT!"

Q  What happens when you put a tooth into a glass of water?

"Not now, Terry," I say. "This is no time for jokes—my tooth is hurting too much!"

"I know that," he says, "but your tooth is the solution to our problem."

"How do you figure that?" I say.

"All we need to do is pull it out," says Terry, "and then you can leave it out tonight for the tooth fairy, and you will get two dollars for it and then we'll have enough money to buy the Joke Writer 2000™!"

A  It gets wet.

"That's crazy," I say.

"Oh," says Terry, disappointed.

"*So* crazy it just might work!" I say. "Let's try it!"

"Yay!" says Terry.

# CHAPTER 6

# TUG-OF-WAR

"Terry Dent*ist* at your service!" says Terry. "Hold still and I'll just knock your tooth out with this hammer."

"No way!" I say. "It's hurting enough already! No hammer!"

"No hammer? No problem!" says Terry. "I'll use this tooth dynamite instead. It says here: *Just put one stick in your mouth near the aching tooth and light the fuse.*"

"DEFINITELY NOT!" I say. "No hammer and no tooth dynamite! The tooth fairy won't want my tooth if it's exploded to bits. You are a *terrible* dentist!"

"Well, I'm all out of ideas then," says Terry. "Maybe we should go and ask the three wise owls how to get your tooth out."

"I don't know about that," I say. "I'm not so sure those owls are as wise as you think they are."

"Do you have any other ideas?" says Terry.

"No," I say with a groan. "Let's go and see the wise owls."

We jet-chair up to the owl house.

"Greetings, O wise owls!" says Terry.

What is an owl's favorite subject?

"Just as I suspected," I say. "This is a waste of time. Let's go."

"No, give them a chance, Andy," says Terry. "We haven't even asked our question yet."

Terry turns to address the owls. "O wise owls! We do beseech thee to tell us the answer to our question: What is the best way to remove Andy's aching tooth?"

"String! Doorknob! Slam!" say the wise owls.

"See?" I say. "I *knew* this wasn't a good idea. They're just hooting random words!"

"No, they're not!" says Terry. "They're making perfect sense. They're telling us that all we have to do is tie a bit of *string* to your tooth, tie the other end to a *doorknob,* and then *slam* the door. The force of the door slamming will pull out your tooth, and all our problems will be solved!"

"Well," I say, "it does sound a little less painful than hammers or dynamite."

"Definitely," says Terry. "And we can get some string from the tangled-up level. Come on!" He turns to the wise owls. "Farewell, O wise ones, and thanks for the wise advice!"

The tangled-up level looks even more tangled-up than usual. It's a big crazy jumble of cords, wires, cables, ribbons, twine, ropes, threads, and string, all tangled together in the biggest tangled-up tangle you've ever seen. There is caution tape around it, but you can't really read it because the caution tape is all tangled up as well.

"I'm going to go in and untangle a bit of string," says Terry.

"All right," I say, "but be careful. It's pretty tangly in there."

"Don't worry, Andy," says Terry. "I'll be really, REALLY careful . . ."

Q What boy wizard magically grew a beard each night?

"Help, Andy!" says Terry. "I'm all tangled up!"

"If only you'd listened to me," I say. "I told you to be careful!"

"I *did* listen to you, and I *was* careful," says Terry. "But I got all tangled up anyway."

"Well, stop struggling," I say. "You're just making it worse. Stay still while I get the emergency detangler."

I grab the detangler, release the safety catch, point the nozzle at Terry, and press the trigger.

Q   How does the man in the moon cut his hair?

The detangler has an instant effect.

Every single bit of string, cord, wire, rope, and thread is detangled—including Terry's hair, which has gone all straight and is hanging down over his face.

"I can't see!" says Terry. "I can't see *anything*! Where has everything *gone*?!"

"Calm down," I say. "It's just your hair. The detangler has straightened out your curls. Come with me to the giant hair dryer and we'll have you back to normal in no time."

A  Eclipse it.

What is good for a bald head?

"Thanks, Andy," says Terry. "That feels *much* better!"

"No problem," I say. "Did you get the string?"

"String?" says Terry. "What string?"

"THE STRING YOU WENT TO THE TANGLED-UP LEVEL TO GET!" I yell.

"Oops," says Terry. "After all the tangling and detangling I kind of forgot. But it doesn't matter. I think there's some string in the kitchen drawer."

"But if you *knew* there was string in the kitchen drawer, why didn't we just get it from there in the first place?"

"Because I forgot," says Terry. "I was having a bad hair day, you know."

"Your bad hair happened *after* you forgot about the string," I say.

"Oh, yeah," says Terry. "I forgot about that, too."

I groan.

"Poor Andy," says Terry. "You sure are in a lot of pain."

"Let's just go to the kitchen," I say.

In the kitchen, Terry opens the third drawer down and pulls out a big ball of string.

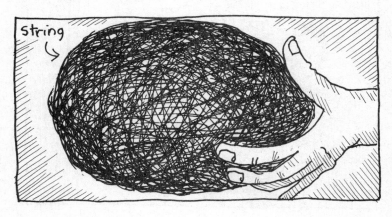

"Open wide, Andy," he says.

I open my mouth and Terry ties one end of the string to my sore tooth . . .

. . . and the other end to the handle of our bathroom door.

Imagine you are in a room with no doors, windows, or anything. How do you get out?

"Okay," says Terry. "Here we go. Ready, set . . . SLAM!"

He slams the door.

When is a door not a door?

When it's ajar.

Q  What lets you walk through walls?

"Is it out?" says Terry.

"No," I say. "And now I've not only got a toothache, I've got a headache as well! This is the worst day ever!"

"Don't despair," says Terry. "I think I know another way to do it, but we're going to need some help."

"It better not involve another door," I say.

"No," says Terry. "Your tooth is too tough for that. It's going to take a full-scale tug-of-war to get it out of your head. Come with me to the forest."

Five minutes later we're in the forest. Terry has tied me to a tree and assembled a huge tug-of-war team, including Bill the postman, Edward Scooperhands, the Trunkinator, and all of Jill's animals.

Moo!

Neigh!

Why did the scientist put a knocker on her door?

Q In what sport do winners go backward and losers go forward?

"Okay," shouts Terry. "Here we go! Ready, set . . . PULL!"

Q What did the dog say to the little child pulling its tail?

Giant rabbit ↓

A "This is the end of me."

"Aarghh!" I scream as my tooth is torn out of my mouth.

Q  What bird is with you at every meal?

The tug-of-war team, surprised by their sudden victory, lose their grip on the string and all fall backward in a big heap. My tooth flies upward, trailing the string behind it . . .

. . . and is snatched by a passing bird!

"Hey!" I say. "That stupid bird just snatched my tooth!"

Q What do you call a seagull when it flies over the bay?

"That's not a stupid bird!" says Jill, peering up at it through her bird-watching binoculars. "That's an extremely rare high-flying, mountain-dwelling worm-snatcher. It must have thought the string was a worm."

"If it can't tell the difference between a bit of string and a worm, then it *is* a stupid bird," I say.

"We've got to get Andy's tooth back," says Terry. "We need it for the tooth fairy!"

"Oh, dear," says Jill, still looking through her binoculars. "I think that's going to be a bit difficult because the bird is heading for its nest high on a rocky, snow-covered crag near the top of Mount Everest."

"Well, we'll just have to climb up and get it then, won't we?" I say.

What is green and pecks on trees?

"But we can't climb Mount Everest!" says Terry. "It's too cold, too high, and too hard. Plus it will take much too long!"

"I'm not suggesting we climb the *mountain*," I say. "We'll take the stairs. Our never-ending staircase goes pretty close to the nest. We can climb up, jump across, and get the tooth—easy!"

"What are we waiting for then?" says Terry. "Let's go!"

"I'll come, too," says Jill. "I've always wanted to see a high-flying, mountain-dwelling worm-snatcher up close!"

Q  Who can jump higher than the highest mountain?

# UP AND UP AND UP

We go to the never-ending staircase and start climbing. We climb up and up and . . .

A   We can, because mountains can't jump.

There is a one-story house where everything is red.

the couch is red, the kitchen is red, the kitchen table is red . . .

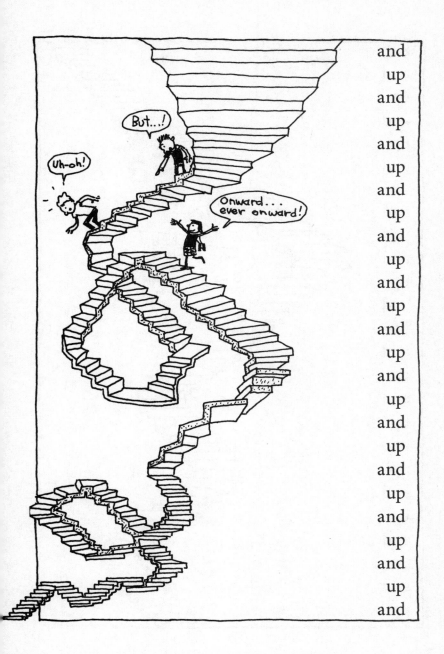

and
up
and
up
and
up
and
up
and
up
and
up
and
up
and
up
and
up
and
up
and
up
and
up
and
up
and

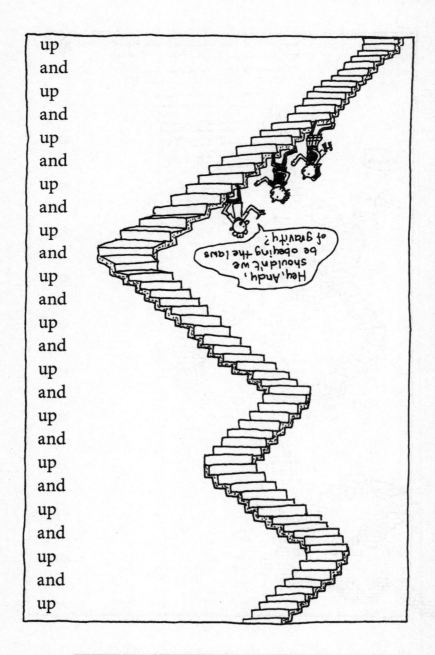

the food inside the fridge is red . . .

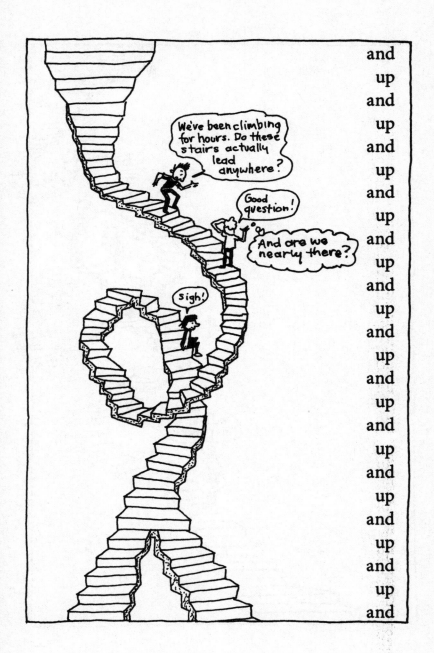

and
up
and
up
and
up
and
up
and
up
and
up
and
up
and
up
and
up
and
up
and
up
and
up
and

up
and
up
and
up
and
up
and
up
and
up
and
up
and
up
and
up
and
up
and
up
and
up
and
up
and
up

the knives are red, the forks are red, the spoons are red . . .

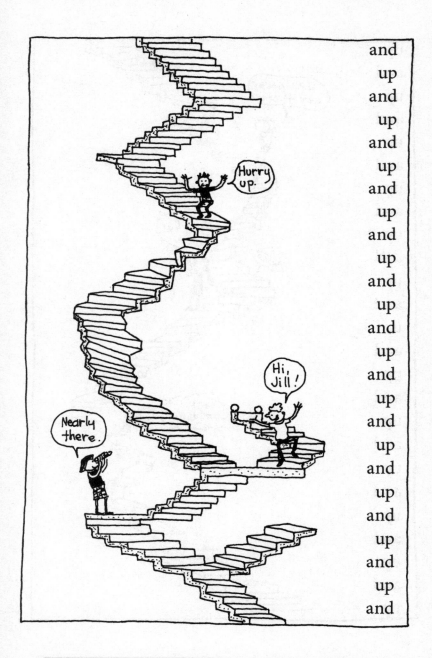

and
up
and
up
and
up
and
up
and
up
and
up
and
up
and
up
and
up
and
up
and
up
and
up
and

the clothes inside them are red—believe it or not, even the dog is red.

and
up
and
up
and
up
and
up
and
up
and
up
and
up
and
up
and
up
and
up
and
up
and
up
and

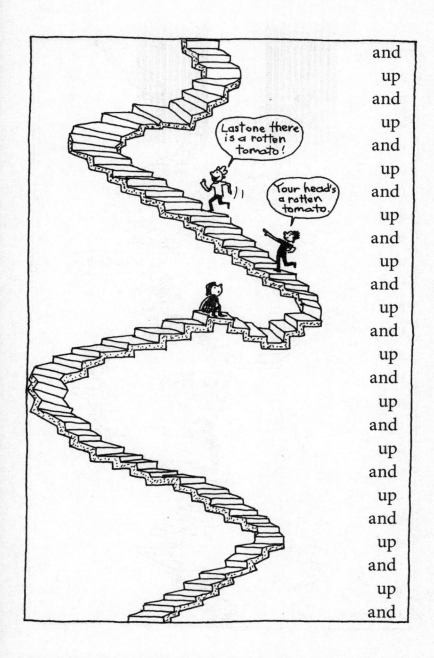

and
up
and
up
and
up
and
up
and
up
and
up
and
up
and
up
and
up
and
up
and
up
and

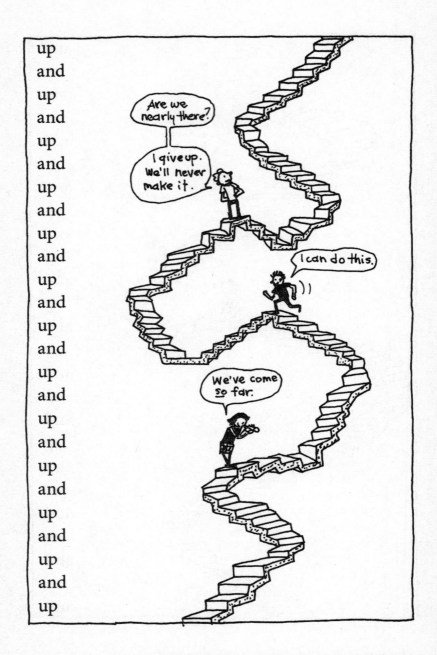

the toilet is red, the toilet water is red, the toilet brush is red . . .

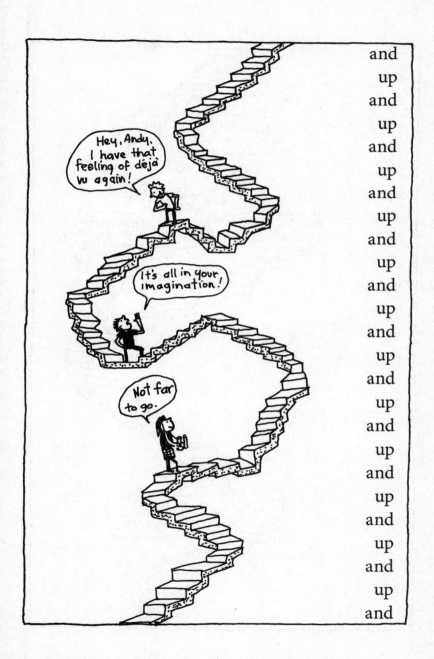

Q the mirrors are red, the sinks are red, the taps are red . . .

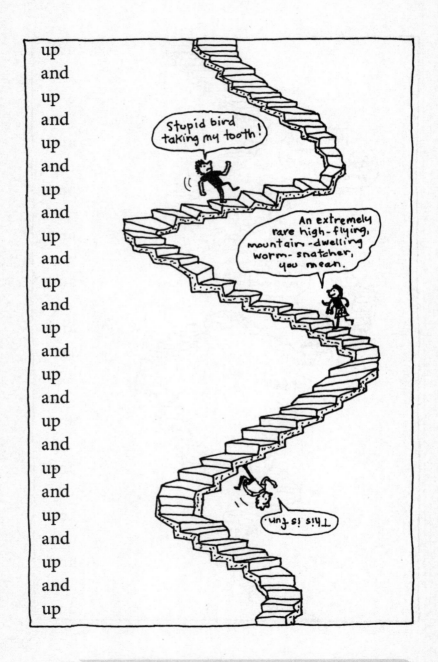

the toothbrushes are red, the toothpaste is red . . .

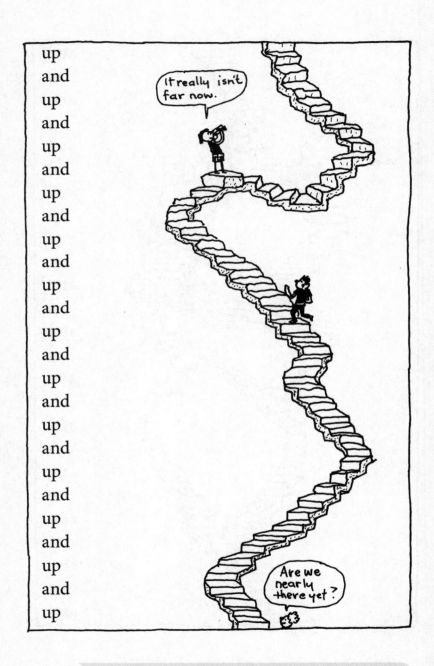

the hallway is red, the air is red . . .

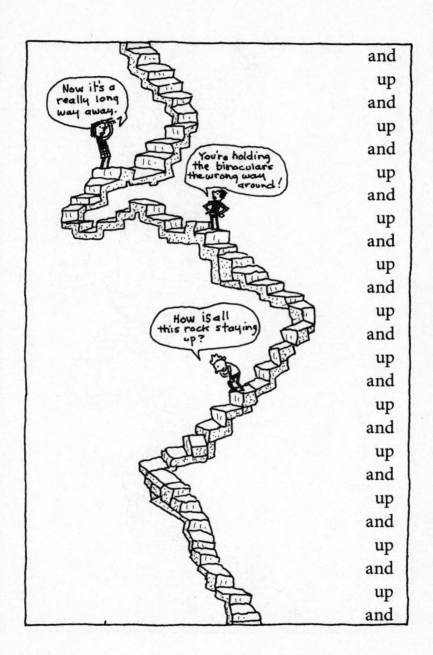

and
up
and
up
and
up
and
up
and
up
and
up
and
up
and
up
and
up
and
up
and
up
and

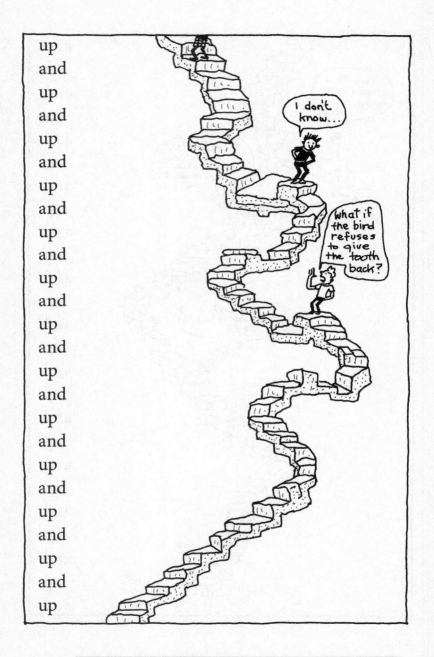

the pages of the books are red, the words are red . . .

up
and
up
and
up
and
up
and
up
and
up
and
up
and
up
and
up
and
up
and
up
and
up
and
up
and
up
and
up

the bookmarks are red, the curtains are red, the dining table is red . . .

and the cat is red, and the canary is red . . .

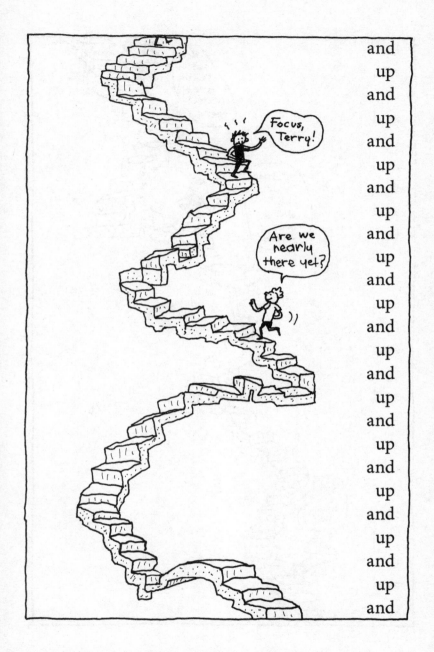

and
up
and
up
and
up
and
up
and
up
and
up
and
up
and
up
and
up
and
up
and
up
and
up
and

and the fish tank is red and the fish in the fish tank are red.

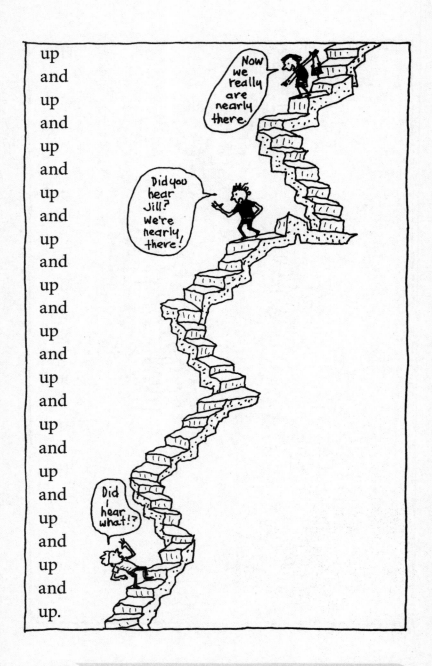

# CHAPTER 8

# PEEP! PEEP! PEEP!

"Are we there yet?" says Terry (for about the fifty millionth time).

"Almost," I say. "Just a few more steps."

"Look," says Jill. "There's the nest!"

"Can you see my tooth?" I say.

"No," says Jill. "Just a bunch of the cutest baby birds I've ever seen!"

A   There are no stairs because it's a one-story house!  

We climb up a few more thousand steps until we are right across from the nest. But there's a big gap between the staircase and the nest. And a *long* drop back down to the ground.

"How are we going to get across?" says Terry. "It's much too far to jump."

"I know," I say. "It didn't look this far when we were looking up at it from the forest."

Why did the golfer wear two pairs of pants?

"What about your emergency inflatable underpants, Terry?" says Jill. "We could whoosh across in those."

"I'm not wearing them," he says. "They got a puncture when we used them to sail to the desert island in the last book. But I *am* wearing my emergency inflatable ears."

A  In case she got a hole in one.

"Are you kidding me?" I say. "Emergency inflatable *ears*?! That's the dumbest thing you've come up with since the Ninja Snail Training Academy."

"Yeah, but my Ninja Snails saved the day," says Terry, "just like my emergency inflatable ears will. Watch this!"

He takes a deep breath, concentrates hard, and then . . .

his ears inflate to about a thousand times their normal size!

What did the earwig say as it fell off the cliff?

"See?" he says. "I told you!"

"You look so cute with big ears," says Jill. "Just like Dumbo the flying elephant!"

"Yeah, he looks dumb all right," I say. "But what use are they?"

"Well," says Terry, "they're flappable and really good for getting from, say, the steps of a never-ending staircase across to, say, a bird's nest. Climb into my ears and I'll take us there right now. Everybody ready? *Ear* we go!"

Terry launches himself from the staircase and starts flapping his ears as fast as he can.

# THE DAY TERRY TURNED INTO AN EARPLANE

Q How do you tell if there is an elephant in your fridge?

"Prepare the cabin for landing," says Terry. "Please ensure tray tables are closed and seats are upright. Thank you for flying with Terry D. *Ear*lines."

"What tray tables?" I say. "What seats? All I had to sit on was this disgusting lump of earwax!"

"Hey!" says Terry. "I heard that!"

Terry lands in the nest with a bump, and Jill and I fall out of his ears.

We are immediately surrounded by a bunch of noisy baby birds, all pecking at us.

Terry's emergency inflatable ears don't stand a chance against the baby birds' sharp beaks.

"Hey, those baby birds just popped my ears!" says Terry.

"Yes, they're very pecky," says Jill.

"I hate pecky birds," I say. "Let's look for my tooth and get out of here as fast as we can."

"I think we may have to put off the tooth-hunt for the moment," says Jill. "Here comes the mother bird!"

"Eeek!" I say. "Its beak looks even sharper and pointier than the baby birds' beaks. And much bigger!"

Peep! Peep!

"Can you talk to it, Jill?" says Terry.

"Not while we're in her nest," says Jill. "If she sees us, she's going to peck first and ask questions later. Worm-snatchers are very protective of their young. We have to hide!"

"But there's nowhere *to* hide!" I say.

"In that case," says Jill, "we'll just have to pretend to be baby birds and hope she doesn't notice."

We crouch down, put our hands on our hips, and move our elbows back and forth.

"Cock-a-doodle-doo!" says Terry.

Q If a rooster laid a brown egg and a white egg, what kind of chicks would hatch?

"You're supposed to be pretending to be a baby *worm-snatcher*, Terry," says Jill. "Not a rooster!"

"Oops," says Terry. "How about this: *Peep! Peep! Peep!*"

"Much better!" says Jill. "I mean, *peep! Peep! Peep!*"

The mother worm-snatcher lands, gripping the side of the nest with her enormous talons. Her beak is full of wriggling, writhing worms.

A  None—roosters can't lay eggs.

The *peep-peep-peep*ing of the baby worm-snatchers is deafening. They all crane their necks to the sky and open their beaks wide. We do the same (except we have mouths, not beaks).

The mother worm-snatcher opens her beak and fresh, wriggling worms come raining down into our open mouths.

Q What do you get if you cross a worm and an elephant?

Erk! My mouth is full of cold, dirty, wriggling worms! Yuck! I'm trying not to chew or swallow them, but it's not easy. It's like they *want* to wriggle down my throat.

But, weirdly, Terry doesn't seem to mind them at all. He's slurping them up like he's eating spaghetti!

A Very big wormholes in your garden.

At last, the mother bird runs out of worms, flaps her enormous wings, and flies away.

"Yuck!" I say, spitting out the worms as fast as I can.

Q What did the worm say to the other worm when he was late getting home?

"Double yuck!" says Jill, spitting hers out, too.
"No offense to worms."

Terry doesn't spit his out, though. His mouth
is still full—so full, in fact, that there's a worm
hanging out of it.

One of the baby worm-snatchers snatches the end of the worm and starts pulling on it.

Terry pulls back.

The bird pulls harder.

Terry pulls harder.

"Look at this, Jill," I say. "Terry is having a tug-of-worm with a baby bird."

"Oh, come on, Terry," says Jill. "Let the baby bird have the worm."

"But it's *my* worm," Terry mumbles through a mouthful of worm. "Mother gave it to *me!*"

While Terry is talking, the baby bird seizes its chance, snatching the worm and swallowing it in one greedy gulp.

"Hey!" says Terry. "That's not fair!"

"Yes, it is," says Jill, "because you're not *really* a baby bird and that mother bird was not *really* your mother."

"I know," sighs Terry. "But I am *really* hungry."

"So am I!" I say. "But it doesn't change the fact that worms taste awful. I mean, that baby worm-snatcher over there is getting sick. Not even worm-snatchers like worms!"

How do you tell which end of a worm is which?

"It's not getting *sick*," says Jill. "It's *choking*! It must have tried to eat too many worms at once. Stand back, I'm going to perform the *Wormlich* maneuver!"

GASP!

Jill picks up the bird, holds it upside down, and squeezes it gently.

A Tickle it in the middle and see which end laughs.

The bird coughs up a bunch of worms, including one with a really big white head and an extremely thin body. In fact, it doesn't look so much like a worm as a piece of string. A piece of string that is attached to . . .

. . . MY TOOTH!

"I found my tooth!" I say.

"That must be what it was choking on," says Jill.

Q What do you give a sick bird?

"Yay!" says Terry. "Now all our problems are solved."

"Well, not all of them," I say. "We're still stuck in a nest on the top of Mount Everest with no way of getting down."

"Oh, yeah," says Terry. "But hang on . . . worms are really stretchy. When the mother bird comes back with another load of worms, we could tie them all together and make a worm-bungee to lower us safely back down to the ground."

A Tweetment.

"We can't do that!" says Jill. "That's cruelty to worms!"

"Maybe," says Terry, "but we'd be saving them from being eaten by birds, so we'd sort of be doing them a favor."

"No, we wouldn't," says Jill. "Birds eating worms is nature's way; tying worms together to make a worm-bungee is not."

At that moment we hear the sound of flapping wings and a mighty *RAWK*. We all turn around. The mother worm-snatcher is back—and she's seen us!

She dips her head down and swoops toward us.

"So long, Andy and Jill!" says Terry. "It's been nice knowing you."

"You too," says Jill. "And you too, Andy."

But before I can reply, the baby bird that Jill saved flutters in between us and the mother bird. It *peep-peep-peep*s loudly and quickly.

Q  What bird movie won an Oscar?

"What's happening, Jill?" says Terry. "What's the baby bird saying?"

"It's telling its mother how we saved it from choking," says Jill.

The mother bird turns to us. "RAWK! RAWK! RAWK!" she rawks.

"What does that mean, Jill?" I say. "Is it good or bad?"

"It's good," says Jill. "*Very* good. She says she is extremely grateful and that if there's ever anything she can do to repay us for our quick thinking and kindness, we only have to ask."

"Do you think she could give us a lift back down to the treehouse?" I say.

"I'll ask her," says Jill. She turns to the mother bird. "Rawk, rawk, rawk, rawk?"

The mother bird rawks back at her.

"She says yes, she'd be happy to," says Jill.

A   A bird that will talk your ear off.

We climb up onto the mother bird's back. The feathers are hard and slippery and very difficult to hold on to.

"We can use the string as a set of reins," says Jill, throwing it around the bird's neck. "Everybody ready? Let's fly!"

The worm-snatcher flaps her wings, lifts off from the nest, and begins a rapid descent.

Down
and
down
and
down
we
fly.

Down
and
down
and
down
and
down
and
down
and
down
and
down
and
down
and
down
and
down
and
down
and
down
and
down
and
down
and
down
and
down

Q  What is the most uncomfortable of all birds?

and
down
and
down
and
down
and
down
and
down
and
down
and
down
and
down
and
down
and
down
and
down
and
down
and
down
and

A A wedgie-tailed eagle.

down
and
down
and
down
and
down
and
down
and
down
and
down
and
down
and
down
and
down
and
down
and
down
and
down
and
down
and
down
and
down

Q Which bird is always out of breath?

and
down
and
down
and
down
and
down
and
down
and
down
and
down
and
down
and
down
and
down
and
down
and
down
and
down
and

down
and
down
and
down
and
down
and
down
and
down
and
down
and
down
and
down
and
down
and
down
and
down
and
down
and
down

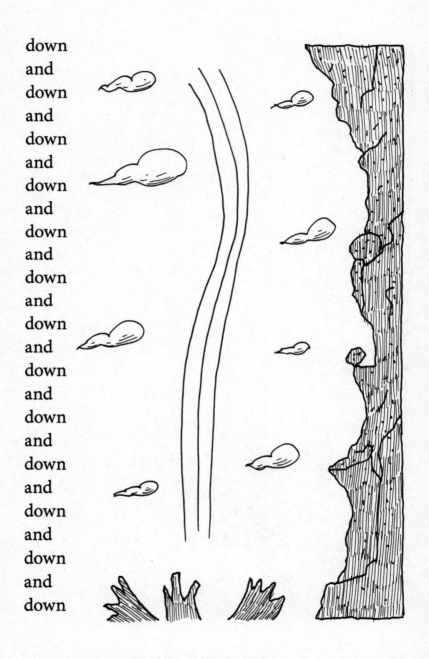

Q  What is a bird's favorite part of the TV news?

and down until we reach the ground. We climb off the bird, and Jill thanks her.

They have a long rawking conversation and then the bird rawks gratefully at us one last time and takes off again.

"What were you and the bird rawking about?" I say.

"She said that if we ever needed her help again, all we have to do is rawk," says Jill. "What a big adventure we've had! I'm going to go straight home and tell my animals all about it."

Q Why did the bird bring toilet paper to the party?

CHAPTER 9

# TERRY, WILL YOU PLEASE BE QUIET, PLEASE?

"Well, I sure am glad that's over," I say. "Now that I've got my tooth back, I'm going to go to bed right away so the tooth fairy can come and give me two dollars!"

A  Because it was a party pooper.

"But it's *way* too early to go to bed," says Terry. "It's still daytime."

"I know," I say, "but I can't wait until tonight—we have to get our book done before then. So can you please be *really* quiet so I can get to sleep?"

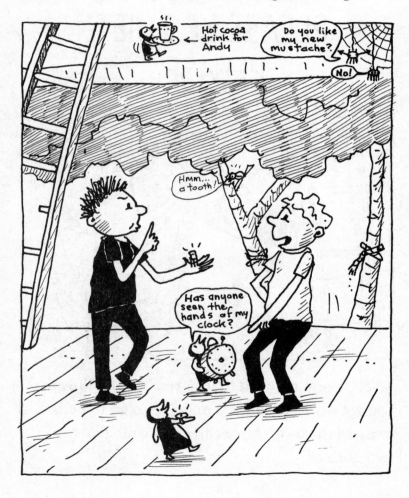

Q  Why does a dragon sleep all day?

"Sure thing, Andy," says Terry. "You can count on me! Good night!"

"Good night, Terry," I say.

I climb the ladder to my bedroom, put on my pajamas, and get into bed.

I am actually feeling quite tired after climbing the never-ending staircase, so I don't think it's going to be too difficult to fall asleep. In fact, I'm falling asleep right now.

I'm falling . . .

falling . . .

falling . . .

falling . . .

falling . . .

falling . . .

CLOMP!

I'm almost asleep when I hear really loud clomping. It's so loud, my bed is shaking.

Q Where do books sleep?

I get out of bed, look over the edge, and see Terry clomping around in a gigantic pair of clomping boots!

"Hey, Terry," I yell. "Quit clomping, will you? I'm trying to get to sleep!"

"Sorry, Andy!" he says. "I was just testing these new, extra-loud clomping boots I invented. Turns out they're even louder than I expected. But I'll take them off now. I won't disturb you again, I promise."

"You'd better not!" I say. "GOOD NIGHT!"

"Good night, Andy," says Terry.

I go back to bed and try to fall asleep again.

I'm falling . . .

falling . . .

falling . . .

falling . . .

falling . . .

falling . . .

GRANGLE!

I'm almost asleep when I hear some of the loudest—
and most ridiculous—noises I've ever heard.

# PARRP! BLEEK! SPROING!

Q How do you get a baby astronaut to sleep?

I get out of bed, look over the edge, and see Terry wearing an extra-stupid, superloud hat!

"Terry!" I yell, but he can't hear me over the deafening noise of his stupid hat.

"TERRY!" I yell again, even louder.

But he still can't hear me.

"TERRY!" I yell as loud as I can.

LOUD-SHOUTING
MARKS
↓

This time he hears me.

"Sorry, Andy," he says. "I couldn't hear you over the noise of this extra-stupid, superloud hat. What's the matter?"

"Your extra-stupid, superloud hat is the matter!" I say. "I'm trying to get to sleep, remember?"

"Oh, sorry, Andy," says Terry. "I forgot. I'll take it off and be very, very quiet from now on. I promise."

"You'd better be," I say. "OR ELSE!"

A  "You wait here, I'll go on a head."

I go back to bed and start falling asleep for the third time.

I'm falling . . .

falling . . .

falling . . .

falling . . .

falling . . .

Q  Why did the girl tiptoe past the medicine cabinet?

falling . . .

falling . . .

falling . . .

falling . . .

I get out of bed, look over the edge, and see Terry playing drums, Superfinger playing guitar, and the Trunkinator dancing in an extra-large pair of extra-loud clomping boots . . .

Q What's the best present you can receive for Christmas?

. . . and to make it even worse, they're all wearing extra-stupid, superloud hats!

Right! That does it! I take a deep breath and yell . . .

# TERRY, PLEASE QU PL

Q  What breaks every time you name it?

# WILL YOU BE IET, EASE?!

"Sorry, Andy," says Terry. "We were just practicing our act for the Treehouse Talent Quest."

"What Treehouse Talent Quest?" I say.

"The one I thought we could have after this book is finished."

"This book won't *be* finished," I say, "if you don't let me get to sleep!!!"

Did you hear about the soldier who bought a camouflage sleeping bag?

"I'll be quiet now," says Terry. "I promise."

"That's what you said last time!" I say.

"I know," says Terry, "but it won't happen again, I really promise. I'll be as quiet as a mouse."

"All right," I say. "Good night . . . *for the last time!*"

I go back to bed and start falling asleep . . .

falling . . .

falling . . .

falling . . .

A  He can't find it.

... asleep.

Q   Why couldn't Dracula's wife go to sleep?

# TERRY AND THE TOOTH FAIRY

'Twas the day of the toothache, when all
through the tree
Not a creature was stirring—no, not even me.
Andy's tooth had been placed
In a small glass with care
In the hopes that the tooth fairy soon would
be there.

A   Because of his coffin.

Andy was nestled all snug in his bed,
While visions of gold coins danced in his head.

And me in the bathtub, blowing a bubble,
Trying my hardest to stay out of trouble.*

*And be really, really quiet!

What TV show should you watch in the bath?

When out in the forest there arose
    such a clatter,
I sprang from my bath to see what
    was the matter.
A towel wrapped around me, I flew
    like a breeze,
To the edge of the deck and peered
    through the leaves.

A  A soap opera.

And what to my wondering eyes should appear,
But a little steam-powered machine
    drawing near.
And a tiny toy truck with a miniature crane,
From which dangled a hook on a small
    golden chain.

Q   What has garbage and flies?

All led by a figure, so lively and airy,
I knew in a moment it must be the tooth fairy!
More rapid than eagles to the treehouse
  she came,
And she whistled and shouted and called her
  helpers by name!

A  A garbage truck.

"Come, Achy! Come, Molar! Come, Driller!
Come, Smash!
To the top of the tree! To the bedroom
let's dash!
And we'll heave away, haul away our
pearly prize
For it's teeth that we gather, no matter
the size!"

And up through the treehouse the
    tiny crew flew,
With both their machines and the
    tooth fairy, too.
They parked their small truck on
    Andy's sweet head
And lowered the hook to the glass by his bed.

A Your teeth.

And then with a chant of "Tooth-heave" and
   "Tooth-ho,"
The tooth was brought up from the water below.
It was placed in the truck and tied up
   very tightly.
With gossamer ropes that glistened
   quite brightly.

Q   What does a dentist call his X-rays?

The tooth fairy flittered and fluttered
   with glee.
"Pay him," she said, "his tooth-fairy fee."
The machine began whirring.
It whistled and blew.
And then out of a slot a two-dollar coin
   flew.

Up through the air flew the newly made cash,
Then into the glass it fell with a splash.
"And now," said the fairy, "it's home we
  must dash
To deliver this tooth for the queen's
  birthday bash!"

Q  What game do cats play at birthday parties?

She sprang to the truck, to her team gave a
    whistle,
And away they all flew like the down
    of a thistle.
But I heard her exclaim, as she drove
    out of sight,
"Thanks for the tooth, and to all a good night."

A Mew-sical chairs.

I decided to follow, for to tell you the truth,
I wanted to see what they'd do with the tooth.
Across land, sea, and rivers the fairy
    crew flew
And not far behind them, I also flew, too.

Q   What flies without wings?

For hours and hours, I followed that band
Until, finally, we reached it—the famed
   Fairyland!
The lights of the city were sparkling
   and shining
And fairies galore were all dancing and dining.

The city was holding a great celebration,
A big birthday bash for the queen of
     their nation.
Andy's tooth was unloaded by the fairies
     with care,
Put into a cannon, and shot into the air.

Q    What do clams do on their birthdays?

And though not a good tooth—it was
    badly corroded—
Andy's molar looked great as it BOOMED
    and exploded!
(Who would have thought that a tooth
    with decay
Could produce such a wonderful
    fireworks display?)

A  They shell-ebrate.

THE NIGHT ANDY'S TOOTH WAS SHOT OUT OF A CANNON IN FAIRYLAND

Q What do you get when you cross a dinosaur with fireworks?

The queen thanked the fairies for her
    birthday surprise
And for the amazing display that had dazzled
    her eyes.
And that is the story of Andy's old tooth.
I was there and I saw it and I swear it's
    the truth!

Q   What did one eye say to the other eye?

# LET'S GO SHOPPING!

A  "There's something between us that smells."

"Wake up, Andy!" says Terry, shaking me roughly.
"Andy! Wake up!"

"What is it *now*, Terry?" I say. "You promised to be
*quiet*! I'm trying to get to sleep so the tooth fairy
can come!"

Q  What did the werewolf eat after he had his tooth
fixed?

"You *did* fall asleep!" says Terry. "And the tooth fairy *did* come!"

"Really?" I say.

"Yes," says Terry, picking up the glass. "Look!"

At the bottom of the glass is a shiny, brand-new two-dollar coin.

"It worked!" I say. "We've got the two dollars we need. But how did you know?"

"I saw the whole thing!" says Terry. "They made so much noise I was afraid they were going to wake you up."

"'They'?" I say. "I thought there was only one tooth fairy."

Q  Why does Dracula clean his teeth three times a day?

"There is," says Terry breathlessly, "but she had a whole gang of helpers, and they had a little truck with a crane and a money-making machine just like ours—only it was tiny and it didn't make honey. I followed them back to Fairyland, and I saw them use your tooth as a firework to help celebrate the fairy queen's birthday!"

A  To prevent bat breath.

"Are you sure you didn't fall asleep as well?" I say. "Sounds like you've been dreaming."

"No, it's *true*," says Terry. "You can ask the readers. They were there, too. They saw me see the whole thing!"

"It's not that I don't *believe* you," I say. "But I think I will check with them anyway."

Well, readers, *is* it true? Did Terry really see all that stuff?

Q What is Dracula's favorite fruit?

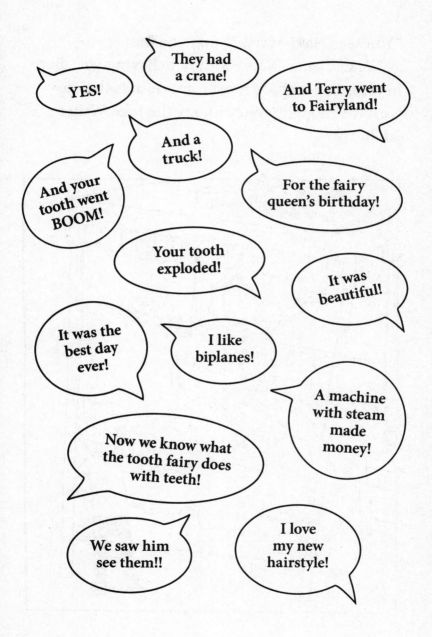

"You see?" says Terry. "I told you!"

"Yeah," I say. "Sorry for not believing you. But never mind—what's most important is that now we have enough money to buy the Joke Writer 2000™!"

Q Where can you always find money?

I get out of bed and get dressed. We grab the rest of our money, jump onto our jet-propelled swivel chairs, and fly as fast as we can to the Two-Million-Dollar Shop.

A  In the dictionary.

"Ah, I was wondering when you'd be back," says Fancy Fish.

"Do you still have the Joke Writer 2000™?" says Terry.

"Yes," says Fancy Fish, "but there's been a lot of interest since you left. You're *very* lucky it's still available."

"We'll buy it!" I say.

"An excellent decision, sir," says Fancy Fish. "Would you like it gift wrapped? I have some very fancy wrapping paper for only two million dollars: the finest-quality wrapping paper in the land—or in the sea!"

Q  What kind of ant is really good at mathematics?

"No, thanks," I say. "It's not a gift; it's for us—we need it for our book."

"As you please," says Fancy Fish, putting his fin out. "That will be four million dollars, please."

"*Four* million dollars?" says Terry.

"Yes, that is correct," says Fancy Fish.

"But it was only *two* million dollars before," I say.

"I know," says Fancy Fish, shrugging, "but since then the price has gone up."

"But this is the *Two*-Million-Dollar Shop," I say.

"Exactly!" he says. "Nothing *under* two million dollars. That's our promise to you."

"But you can't just double the price of something for no reason," says Terry.

"I think you'll find I can," says Fancy Fish, pointing to a sign above the counter.

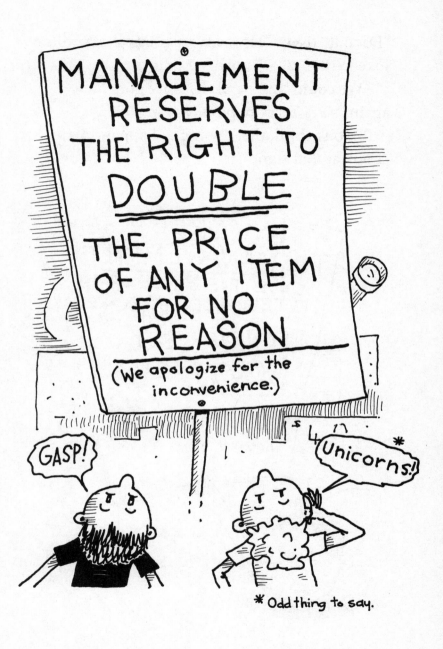

"Darn it!" I say. "How are we going to afford the Joke Writer 2000™ now?"

"We could wait until the price goes *down* again," says Terry hopefully.

"I don't think that's going to happen," I say. "Look at *that* sign."

Q  How much money does a skunk have?

"This shop is too expensive," says Terry. "I wish we'd never put it in our treehouse."

"Me too," I say. "But on the other hand, it's the *only* shop where we can buy a Joke Writer 2000™, and we *need* a Joke Writer 2000™!"

"Yeah, I know," says Terry. "I guess we're just going to have to find *another* two million dollars. Maybe we could pull out some more of your teeth. The fairy queen was very happy with your last tooth. Perhaps the tooth fairy would pay us *more* than two dollars per tooth—especially if we explained the situation."

"No way!" I say. "You are not pulling out any more of my teeth! Besides, I've got a *much* better idea."

"What is it?" says Terry.

"We can go to the Two-Dollar Shop and use my new two-dollar coin to buy another two million dollars. Then we'll have *four* million dollars and we can come back and buy the Joke Writer 2000™!"

"Wow," says Terry, "you are getting *much* better at math, Andy! But you've made a slight miscalculation. If we use your two dollars to buy two *million* dollars, we'll still be two dollars short, so we need to buy two million and *two* dollars."

"Oh, yeah," I say.

I turn to Fancy Fish. "Hold that Joke Writer 2000™! We'll be right back!"

We rush to the Two-Dollar Shop. When we arrive, Pinchy McPhee is out front beside a big pile of money and a MONEY SALE sign.

Q If there are four dollars and you take away three, how many do you have?

"We're in luck, Andy!" says Terry. "Pinchy is having a money sale! All the money is only two dollars! This is the *best* value shop in the whole treehouse!"

I'm rich!

He's rich.

MONE SALE

"You're right about that!" says Pinchy. "How can I help you?"

"We'd like to buy two million and two dollars, please," I say.

A  You took three dollars, so obviously you have three.

"Certainly," says Pinchy. He grabs a big pile of cash and puts it on the counter.

"There you go," he says. "Two million and two dollars! That will be two dollars, please. Would you like that gift wrapped?"

Q What do giraffes have that no other animal has?

"No, thanks," I say. "It's not a gift; it's for us—we need it to buy a Joke Writer 2000™ for our book."

I hand over my new two-dollar coin. "Thanks, Pinchy!"

"Thank *you*," says Pinchy, pinching the shiny gold coin in his pincer. "I think I feel a song coming on!"

"Uh-oh," whispers Terry. "Let's get out of here!"

MONEY SALE!
ANY AMOUNT OF MONEY
NO MATTER HOW LARGE or SMALL
YOB ONLY
$2

When we get back to the Two-Million-Dollar Shop, Fancy Fish is waiting for us, still holding the Joke Writer 2000™ in his fin.

"Well?" he says. "What's your decision?"

"We'll buy it!" I say.

"Wonderful," says Fancy Fish. "That will be eight million dollars, please!"

Q  What do you call a fish with no eyes?

"WHAT?!" I say. "*EIGHT* MILLION DOLLARS?!"

"YOU CAN'T DOUBLE THE PRICE AGAIN!" says Terry. "IT'S NOT RIGHT AND IT'S NOT *FAIR!*"

"Relax," says Fancy Fish. "Keep your scales on! I was just having a little joke. The price is still four million dollars."

"Phew!" says Terry as we dump the money on the counter. "For a moment there I thought we were going to have to go back to the Two-Dollar Shop and buy even *more* money!"

Fancy Fish sweeps all the money off the counter with a swift swish of his fancy fins and then puts the Joke Writer 2000™ in my hand. I immediately feel 110 percent funnier. This book is going to be good. This book is going to be great. This book is going to be the goodest, greatest, funniest book we have ever written!

Q What do you get when you cross a fish and a kitten?

# CHAPTER 12

# JOKE-WRITING TIME

Before we can start work, however, we really need to eat. After all that stair-climbing and sleeping and shopping, both Terry and I are feeling pretty hungry.

A A purr-anha.

The marshmallow machine senses our hunger and starts firing marshmallows into our mouths at high speed.

Q Why did the elephant stand on the marshmallow?

"I'm full!" I say.

"Me too," says Terry.

We close our mouths. The marshmallow machine keeps firing marshmallows at our faces for a while and then drifts away to see if anybody else in the treehouse is hungry.

"Right," I say. "*Now* we can get started."

I pick up the Joke Writer 2000™. It's surprisingly heavy, and for a moment I wonder how I'm actually going to write with it, but then something incredible happens—it leaps out of my hand and starts writing all by itself!

"Look, Terry!" I say. "It's writing automatically! I'm not doing *anything*!"

"Wow!" says Terry. "That's amazing! It's doing all the work. I can't wait to see why the koala fell out of the tree. I bet it will be hilarious."

"Well, you won't have to wait long," I say. "It's writing the answer right now!"

"I was right," says Terry. "It *is* hilarious! Make it write another one."

I put the tip of the Joke Writer 2000™ on the paper, and it starts writing again.

Q   What do you get if you cross a lemon and a cat?

"That's even funnier than the first one," says Terry.

"I know!" I say. "This pencil is fantastic!"

"Can I have a go?" says Terry.

"Sure," I say, passing it to him.

Terry puts the tip of the pencil on the paper. It breaks free of his grip and takes off again.

Terry laughs so hard, he snorts milk out of his nose—and he's not even drinking milk!

"Oh, boy," says Terry. "This pencil is amazing!"

"I know," I say. "With a pencil *this* funny, we'll be able to write the funniest books ever!"

Q What do cows give after an earthquake?

"The Joke Writer 2000™ is worth every single dollar we paid for it," says Terry.

"It sure is," I say. "It's worth every bun that knocked us backward, every flying fridge that almost flattened us, every single stair we climbed on the never-ending staircase, and every slimy, revolting, wriggling worm we ate in the worm-snatcher's nest. It's the greatest pencil ever!"

A Milkshakes.

As we stand there admiring the Joke Writer 2000™, we see a bird flying toward us.

"Hey, that looks like the worm-snatcher," says Terry.

"Sort of," I say, "but it's the wrong color."

Suddenly the bird dives at great speed, snatches the Joke Writer 2000™ out of Terry's hand, and takes off, back up into the sky.

"Oh, no," says Terry, "not again!"

We are just standing there—stunned—when Jill pokes her head and shoulders up through the branches, her binoculars around her neck.

"Did you just see a high-flying, mountain-dwelling Joke Writer–snatcher come through here?" she says. "I lost track of it when it dived into the treehouse."

Q  Why did the robber take a bath?

"We saw it all right!" I say. "It just swooped down here and snatched our Joke Writer 2000™!"

"They do that," says Jill. "That's why they're called Joke Writer–snatchers."

"Don't tell me we have to climb the never-ending staircase up to Mount Everest *again*," says Terry.

"No," I say. "Actually, I don't think we do. And you know what? I'm not sure that we needed to climb it in the first place."

"Yes, we did," says Terry. "We needed to get your tooth."

"I know we *thought* we did," I say, "but I've just realized that after you pulled my tooth out back in chapter six I haven't had any toothache, so I don't really need the Joke Writer 2000™ to help me write."

Terry frowns. "So if we didn't need to climb the never-ending staircase to get your tooth," he says, "does that mean we didn't need to pretend to be baby birds and eat all those worms?"

Q  Why did the chicken cross the road and then cross back again?

"Well, you didn't have to eat quite so *many* worms,"
I say. "But no, we didn't need to do that, either."

"And I didn't need to be really quiet so you
could go to sleep and the tooth fairy would come?"

"No," I say.

"That means I had a bath for nothing!" says Terry.
"And we spent *four million dollars* on a joke-
writing pencil that we only got three jokes out of.
We could have bought the solid-gold toilet seat
after all! And now we don't have any money left!"

A   Because it was a double-crosser.

"I know," I say, "but it is *kind* of funny when you think about it."

Terry thinks about it. And then he thinks about it some more. He frowns—and then he laughs. "You're right," he says. "It *is* pretty funny that we did all that stuff we didn't even need to do."

Jill laughs, too. "And look on the bright side," she says. "It's going to make a great story for your book."

"Yeah!" says Terry. "Especially now Andy's got his sense of humor back!"

"I sure have," I say. "I'm feeling funny enough to write the book *and* all the jokes . . . with your help, of course."

"And mine!" says Jill. "I know lots of *animal* jokes. Listen to this one: What do you call a sleeping dinosaur?"

"I don't know," I say. "What?"

"A dino-snore!" says Jill.

"That joke is not only funny, it's *true*!" says Terry. "Let's get started right away!"

So we write . . .

and we draw . . .

and we draw . . .

and we write . . .

A A pigpen.

and we draw . . .

and we write . . .

and we write . . .

and we draw . . .

and we draw . . .

and we write . . .

Q   Why is a raven like a writing desk?

and we draw . . .

and we write . . .

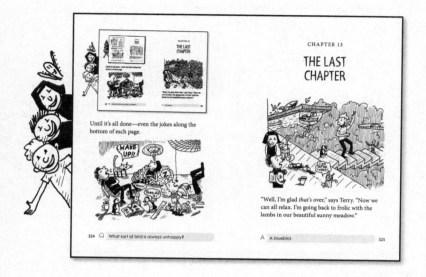

Until it's all done—even the jokes along the bottom of each page.

**Q** What sort of bird is always unhappy?

# THE LAST CHAPTER

"Well, I'm glad *that's* over," says Terry. "Now we can all relax. I'm going back to frolic with the lambs in our beautiful sunny meadow."

A  A bluebird.

"And I'm going to keep tracking that high-flying, mountain-dwelling Joke Writer–snatcher," says Jill. "They are such fascinating creatures. They're even more rare than high-flying, mountain-dwelling worm-snatchers!"

"Hey, not so fast, you two!" I say. "Aren't you forgetting something?"

"No, I don't think so," says Terry.

"No, I can't think of anything, either," says Jill.

"Okay, then let me ask each of you a riddle," I say.

"Oh, goody," says Terry. "I love riddles!"

"All right," I say. "Terry's riddle first. What's big and red and gets bigger and redder the angrier it gets and then explodes if a certain writer and illustrator don't get their book delivered by two thirty today?"

"Hmmm," says Terry, scratching his chin. "Beats me."

"MR. BIG NOSE'S NOSE!" I yell.

"Yikes!" says Terry. "But it's already two twenty-five! How are we going to get our book to him on time?"

"I don't know!" I say. "But we'd better figure something out . . . and fast!"

Mr. Big Nose! Of course!!

"Hang on," says Jill. "What's my riddle? You said you had one for me, too."

Me next!

Then me.

"I sure do," I say. "What has one hundred heads, four hundred legs, lots of fur, and is about to go to sleep for six months?"

"Oh, my goodness!" says Jill. "The answer is *one hundred bears*! We promised to read them your book before they go to sleep. You have to deliver it to Mr. Big Nose or those poor bears will have to go into hibernation without their bear-time story!"

What has 100 heads, 400 legs, and is about to go to sleep for six months?

"I know!" I say. "But how are we going to get our book to Mr. Big Nose?"

"We could ask the high-flying, mountain-dwelling worm-snatcher to take us," says Jill. "She promised she would help us whenever we were in need, and we are definitely *in need* right now!"

"Let's call her," I say. "Everybody ready? On the count of three: one . . . two . . . three!"

Q Two silkworms were in a race. Who won?

We've barely had time to close our mouths when the worm-snatcher swoops down, snatches us all up in her mighty talons . . .

. . . and carries us off to Mr. Big Nose's office.

A   It was a tie.

# THE DAY THE HIGH-FLYING, MOUNTAIN-DWELLING WORM-SNATCHER SNATCHE US ALL UP AND FLEW US TO MR. BIG NOSE'S OFFICE

Q  What can travel around the world while staying in a corner?

A A stamp.

Luckily for us, Mr. Big Nose's office window is open. The worm-snatcher releases us at just the right moment and we all tumble into Mr. Big Nose's office at exactly 2:30 p.m.

"At last!" shouts Mr. Big Nose as we pick ourselves up off the floor and gather up the pages of our book. "I was just about to cancel your contract."

Q What has words but never speaks?

"Sorry, Mr. Big Nose," I say as I hand him the pages. "But we've been very busy. You can read all about it in *The 104-Story Treehouse*. Here it is!"

"Is it as good as the last one?" says Mr. Big Nose. "It had better be!"

"Oh, it is," says Jill. "It's a great story. Possibly the greatest story ever told."

A A book.

"Hmmm," says Mr. Big Nose. "I'll be the judge of that! Well, what are you all standing there for? You can go now. I've got work to do. And so have you—don't forget you have a deadline for next year's book."

"We won't forget," I say. "But before we go, we were wondering if you would be able to do us a very special favor."

"That depends on what it is," says Mr. Big Nose. "I'm a very busy man, you know."

Q What's a frog's favorite year?

"We know," I say, "but would it be possible to put our new book into superfast production so we can take a copy to read to some bears before they go into hibernation? You see, we promised them we would in exchange for them agreeing to leave the treehouse so we could write the book."

"Hmmm," says Mr. Big Nose. "It's highly irregular, but I suppose a promise is a promise—especially where bears are concerned. Wait there, and I'll see what I can do."

Q What do snowmen eat for breakfast?

"Here you are," says Mr. Big Nose. "One freshly printed copy of your new book."

"Thank you, Mr. Big Nose," I say. "We really appreciate it—and so will the bears."

"Let's call the worm-snatcher to take us to the bears' cave," says Jill. "There's not a moment to lose. Winter is almost here!"

Q What is the best way to win a race?

Once again the worm-snatcher appears and snatches us all up, along with our new book.

# THE DAY THE HIGH-FLYING, SNATCHER SNATCHED US UP AND FLEW US TO THE BEARS'

Q What do you call an angry bear?

MOUNTAIN-DWELLING WORM—
FROM MR. BIG NOSE'S OFFICE
CAVE

A  Nothing, just run.

When we arrive, the bears are all in their pajamas, sitting up in a 100-bear bed.

Q  What did the blanket say to the mattress?

They let out a huge 100-bear roar.

"That means, 'Hooray for Andy, Terry, and Jill!'" says Jill.

Terry, Jill, and I sit down in a big chair, get cozy, and start reading to the bears.

Q   What's the last thing you take off before bed?

A few hours later I finally reach this, the last page (just like you), but nobody is listening (except for you, of course). All the bears—and Terry and Jill—are fast asleep.

I've got to admit, I'm feeling pretty sleepy myself. I might just nap for a little while—well, probably most of winter to tell you the truth—and then Terry and I will get busy adding another thirteen new stories to the treehouse. Good night!

## THE END

# RACE TIME

Who do you think would be the fastest? Order them from 1 to 12, with the slowest being 1 and the fastest being 12.

Ninja Snail

Ninja Snail on a skateboard

Sloth

Cheetah with four broken legs

Cow on a bicycle

Block of wood

Turbo tortoise

Gibbon on a wire

354

☐ Octopus on roller skates

☐ Cow in a Ferrari

VAROOM!

☐ Penguin being chased by the police

POLICE

☐ Elephant on a scooter being chased by a mouse

# MR. BIG NOSE WORD SEARCH

When you've finished there should be 13 letters left over that spell out something to do with Mr. Big Nose.

## WORD LIST

| | | |
|---|---|---|
| AUTHORS | DEADLINES | RED |
| BOOKS | DESK | TEMPER |
| CHAIR | MR BIG NOSE | TIME |
| CLOCK | OFFICE | WINDOW |
| CONTRACTS | PUBLISHER | |

```
M  R  B  I  G  N  O  S  E  B
P  O  F  F  I  C  E  I  H  O
U  A  V  R  E  P  M  E  T  O
B  A  U  T  H  O  R  S  R  K
L  K  E  T  I  M  E  A  I  S
I  S  B  I  G  R  E  D  A  N
S  E  W  O  D  N  I  W  H  O
H  D  S  K  C  O  L  C  C  E
E  C  O  N  T  R  A  C  T  S
R  D  E  A  D  L  I  N  E  S
```

SOLUTION: _ _ _ _ _ _ _ _ _ _ _ _ _

Answers are on page 358.

# SPY COWS

# MR. BIG NOSE WORD SEARCH (PAGE 356)

```
M R B I G N O S E   B
P O F F I C E I H   O
U A V R E P M E T   O
B A U T H O R S R   K
L K E T I M E A I   S
I S B I G R E D A   N
S E W O D N I W H   O
H D S K C O L C C   E
E C O N T R A C T S
R D E A D L I N E S
```

Solution: I HAVE A BIG NOSE

Andy Griffiths lives in a 104-story treehouse with his friend Terry, and together they make funny books, just like the one you're holding in your hands right now. Andy writes the words, and Terry draws the pictures. If you'd like to know more, read this book (or visit www.andygriffiths.com.au).

Terry Denton lives in a 104-story treehouse with his friend Andy, and together they make funny books, just like the one you're holding in your hands right now. Terry draws the pictures, and Andy writes the words. If you'd like to know more, read this book (or visit www.terrydenton.com).

Thank you for reading this FEIWEL AND FRIENDS book.
The Friends who made

possible are:

Jean Feiwel, Publisher
Liz Szabla, Associate Publisher
Rich Deas, Senior Creative Director
Holly West, Editor
Anna Roberto, Editor
Val Otarod, Associate Editor
Kat Brzozowski, Editor
Alexei Esikoff, Senior Managing Editor
Kim Waymer, Senior Production Manager
Anna Poon, Assistant Editor
Emily Settle, Assistant Editor
Rebecca Syracuse, Associate Designer
Hayley Jozwiak, Managing Editor

Follow us on Facebook or visit us online at mackids.com.
Our books are friends for life.

# KEEP LAUGHING ALONG WITH THE
## *NEW YORK TIMES*–BESTSELLING SERIES
## BY ANDY GRIFFITHS AND TERRY DENTON